Lipstick & Heels

purposeful design®
p u b l i c a t i o n s
A Division of ACSI

Colorado Springs, CO

Purposeful Design Publications is the publishing division of the Association of Christian Schools International (ACSI) and is committed to the ministry of Christian school education, to enable Christian educators and schools worldwide to effectively prepare students for life. As the publisher of textbooks, trade books, and other educational resources within ACSI, Purposeful Design Publications strives to produce biblically sound materials that reflect Christian scholarship and stewardship and that address the identified needs of Christian schools around the world.

Printed in the United States of America
16 15 14 13 12 11 10 09 08    1 2 3 4 5 6 7

Maher, D'Arcy
    *Lipstick & Heels*
    ISBN 978-1-58331-092-2

Designer: Leslie Swift
Illustrator: Noémi Demeter
Editorial team: Mary Endres, Cheryl Chiapperino

Purposeful Design Publications
*A Division of ACSI*
PO Box 65130 • Colorado Springs, CO 80962-5130
Customer Service: 800/367-0798 • Website: www.acsi.org

From the Illustrator

To those parents and educators who are committed to discovering and developing the talents of their young children.

I would like to express my gratitude to many people, among whom I recognize the following: my parents and my teachers (in particular, my kindergarten teacher, who first discovered my talent for drawing and painting, and in so doing changed my attitude toward school). And last but not least, D'Arcy Maher, who not only expressed her appreciation for my talent but also trusted in my ability to use it. D'Arcy has helped me grow just as my kindergarten teacher did when I was four years old.

Noémi Demeter


From the Author

To Dr. Mary Campbell, a worthy mentor who untiringly offers support and provides professional and spiritual counsel. Who can measure the impact of her investment over her lifetime of service?

To J. C. Campbell, a husband and father who has delighted in and supported his wife, a virtuous woman, for nearly fifty years. Dr. Mary accurately describes her husband as a blessing.

To my own husband, Tom Maher, for giving me the greatest gift I've ever received.

To my mom, Barbara Dretke, who did not laugh when I told her, at age eight, that I wanted to write a book—about birds. Instead, she provided me with some inspiration.

Special thanks to: Steve Babbitt, László Demeter, David Scott, Robin Stephenson, and Leslie Swift.

D.L.D.M.

There once was a little girl
who loved little girl things.

She loved to play with lipstick.

She loved to play with paints.

3

She loved to play in high-heeled shoes.

She felt grown-up with lipstick on her lips.

With a paintbrush
in her hands, she
felt like an artist.

She stood tall with **high heels** on her feet, and standing tall, she felt she could do anything.

As she grew up, she never forgot about the things she loved.

When it was finally time for her to decide what to do for a job, she already had an idea.

She wore high heels
and lipstick every day.

But a classroom was just too small for all her ideas.

12

She became a principal, and she helped both teachers and children. She wore high heels and lipstick every day.

Soon she realized that a school was just too small for all her ideas.

She started teaching at a university, where she trained teachers to love children and to love artists.

But even a university was just too small for all her ideas.

She was ready
for a change.

What could be bigger than a university? Where would she go? What would she do? Would she be able to wear high heels and lipstick?

She thought
and she thought
and she thought.

She was stumped.

Then one day
a student called.

RING!

RING!

Then another student called.

24

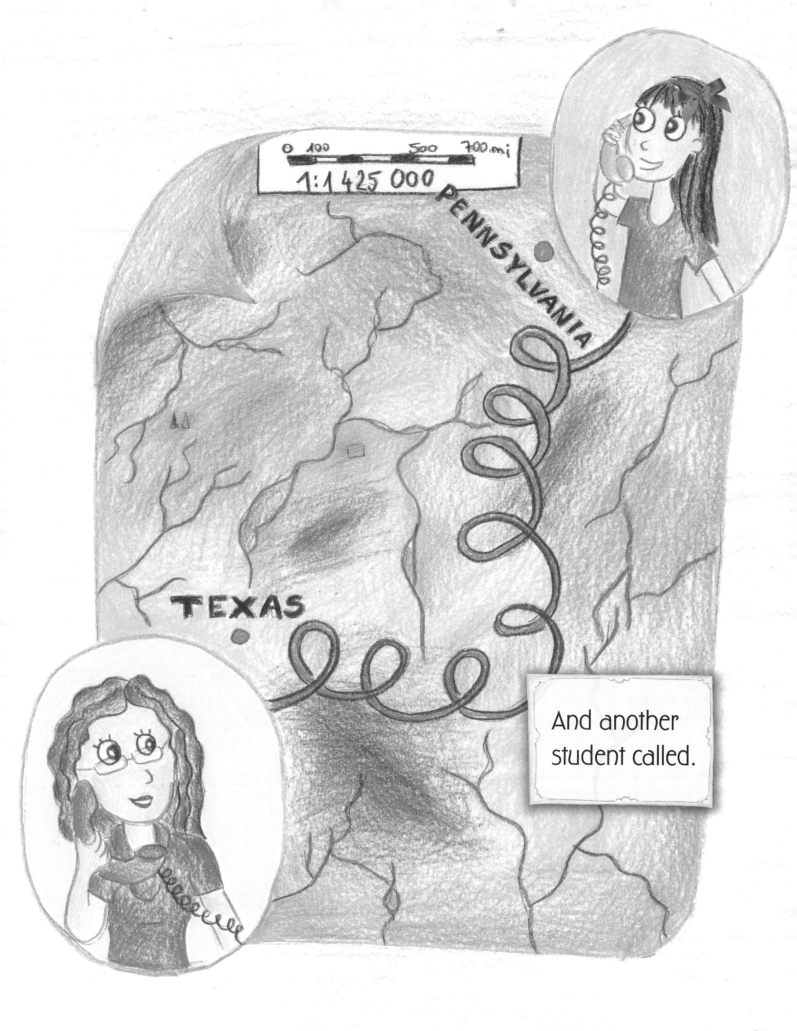

Students and friends called and called. They needed her ideas for all kinds of projects.

Soon she realized that the world was her classroom. It wasn't too big, and it wasn't too small. It was just right.

She still wears lipstick
every day, but she doesn't
have to wear high heels.
She stands tall without them.

Students and colleagues don't believe the world is big enough for her. Only eternity will contain her dreams.

**Dr. Mary Campbell** was selected to be recognized by the Association of Christian Schools International for her contributions to the field of early education throughout her lifetime of service. In an attempt to expand her influence directly into the classroom, this book has been written with the young child in mind. The life of Dr. Campbell has inspired many teachers. This book creates another opportunity for her to inspire young children to dream about how their own gifts and talents can serve others.

With over thirty years of experience in education, Dr. Campbell has served in both public and Christian schools as a teacher and an administrator. She has also served for fourteen years as the Christian education director at Gospel Lighthouse Church. As a guest speaker, Dr. Campbell continues to travel. She has been privileged to minister in several countries and a number of states. She has spoken on education, Christian education, and early childhood education at conferences, conventions, and churches. In addition, Dr. Campbell has written a book on Bible doctrine and has published many articles. She has written Christian education curricula for three publishing companies. She appreciates the visual arts, as well, and is an accomplished artist in her own right.

She has a BA from North Texas State University, an MFA (Masters in Fine Arts) from Southern Methodist University, and a PhD in education from Texas Women's University.

## Meet the Illustrator

Noémi Demeter, age sixteen, is a Hungarian artist who discovered her love for creating at age four. At age thirteen, her illustrations appeared in the Hungarian translation of *Child-Sensitive Teaching*, an early education teacher textbook. Noémi has two brothers and three sisters, and she performs with them each Christmas Eve in a family musical concert. Noémi plays the flute and sings with great proficiency. In Budapest, Noémi attends an art magnet school, where she continues to explore various art mediums and to build her portfolio. She envisions a future of utilizing her gifts to create visual interpretations of texts, events, and fashions.

## Meet the Author

D'Arcy Maher, MEd, serves as the director of early education services for the Association of Christian Schools International. She joined the ACSI team after working in preschools with Washington State Migrant Council and in urban programs in Dallas, Texas. D'Arcy participated in the creation and launching of ACSI's Principles and Practices of Christian Early Education course, and she assisted in setting the protocol for ACSI's preschool accreditation program. She currently serves as the managing editor for *Christian Early Education* magazine and provides support to distance education students as an adjunct professor for Southwestern Assemblies of God University. She loves to read, and she especially enjoys children's literature.

# Extension Activities

Classroom uses for this book:

1. Introduce new vocabulary and provide definitions:
   *artist  job  principal  university*

2. Find the photographs on each page.

3. Use Mary Campbell's story to support thematic units such as these:
   a. God Made Me Special
   b. Careers
   c. Grandparents Day

   For example:

   Explain: This book is about Dr. Mary Campbell, who is a grandparent. What are some of the jobs your grandparents have had? What have they done to help others?

   Assign: Write and illustrate a short picture book about the lives of your grandparents.

4. Tell another story:

   Select a special adult in your program who has a story to tell. Invite the person to tell the story to your class, or prepare the children in advance to interview their guest. Afterward, allow each child to choose a portion of the story to illustrate. Help the children arrange their pages in order so that their illustrations tell the story. Follow book conventions by numbering the pages and including a title page and a dedication page. Finally, when the book is finished, invite the special adult back and let a volunteer present the book to its subject.

5. Explore biblical concepts:

   a. Serving others:
   Mary Campbell trained teachers to love children and to love artists. She shared her ideas.
   Define: *serve* and *serving*.
   Ask the children: Do you have to wait until you're an adult to serve others? What are some ways you can serve your friends and family?

   b. Recognizing that we are all special and that we all have unique, God-given gifts:
   Mary Campbell loved to paint.
   Define: *gifts* and *unique*.
   Ask the children: What are your favorite things to do? What are some things you're very good at doing? How might your special gift make God smile?

6. Consider using this book with one or more Bible stories to expand the discussion:
   a. The boy Samuel—I Samuel 3
   b. Young David: anointed as king—I Samuel 16:1–13; playing the harp—I Samuel 16:14–24; defeating Goliath—I Samuel 17
   c. A boy shares his lunch of five loaves and two fish—John 6:1–15

7. Expand the creative arts area:

   a. As children listen to the story and view the illustrations, they might become eager to create. Allow time for them to create a picture showing themselves doing something they like to do. Once it is finished, ask the artist to explain the drawing or painting to you.

   b. Tell the class that many artists give each of their pictures a title. Help each child choose a title for his or her picture. Write each title on a post-it as the child dictates it, and attach it to the picture. Explain that artists also often sign their work. (Provide examples.) Suggest that the children sign their pictures.

8. Tell more about the artist:

   a. Read to the class the biography of the artist in the front of this book.

   b. Explain: Noémi is Hungarian. Hungary is a country in Eastern Europe. See if you can find it on the map of the world (or on the globe). Noémi speaks Hungarian. You can listen to her read the book, in Hungarian, on the CD in the back of the book.

   c. Noémi began drawing and painting at a young age. What do you like about the pictures in this book? What is your favorite picture? Should Noémi continue drawing, painting, and coloring? How is Noémi using her gift to serve others?

For the teacher:
To be reminded of the biblical importance of children, read chapter 13 in *Too Small to Ignore* by Dr. Wess Stafford, titled "When 'Follow the Leader' Isn't Child's Play."